THE PAPPOUS PLAY

"What's a *pappous*?" asked Walter.

"It's Greek for grandfather," said Tony. "My *pappous* died."

"Oh." Walter didn't know what to say. He had never known anyone who had died. He couldn't imagine life without Grandpa Walt.

"You're lucky you still have yours," said Tony. "We used to play catch. We'd pretend we were doing a double play together."

"I've seen my brother do that," said Walter. "He's Danny the Driver. He's the best hitter on his team. He gives me pointers sometimes."

Tony picked up a bat leaning against a corner. "Can you teach me to hit before tomorrow?"

Bantam Skylark Books you will enjoy
Ask your bookseller for the books you have
missed

THE DINOSAUR PRINCESS AND
OTHER PREHISTORIC RIDDLES
by David A. Adler
ENCYCLOPEDIA BROWN TRACKS
THEM DOWN by Donald J. Sobol
THE GHOST SHOW (Annie K.'s Theater #2)
by Sharon Dennis Wyeth
THE GREAT SCHOOL LUNCH
REBELLION by David Greenberg
THE GREEN SLIME (Skylark Choose Your
Own Adventure #6) by Susan Saunders
I'LL MEET YOU AT THE CUCUMBERS
by Lilian Moore
THE MIGHTY DOLPHIN (Annie K.'s
Theater #4) by Sharon Dennis Wyeth
THE MUFFIN FIEND by Daniel Pinkwater
PETE APATOSAURUS by Nicole Rubel
SON OF FURRY by Jovial Bob Stine
THE TWINS AND THE WILD WEST
(Sweet Valley Kids #10) created by
Francine Pascal

THE NEVER SINK NINE

Tony's Double Play

BY GIBBS DAVIS

Illustrated by
George Ulrich

A BANTAM SKYLARK BOOK®
NEW YORK • TORONTO • LONDON • SYDNEY • AUCKLAND

RL 2, 005–008

TONY'S DOUBLE PLAY
A Bantam Skylark Book / May 1992

*Skylark Books is a registered trademark of Bantam Books,
a division of Bantam Doubleday Dell Publishing Group, Inc.
Registered in
U.S. Patent and Trademark Office and elsewhere.*

All rights reserved.
Text copyright © 1992 by Gibbs Davis.
Cover art and interior illustrations copyright © 1992 by George Ulrich.
*No part of this book may be reproduced or transmitted
in any form or by any means, electronic or mechanical,
including photocopying, recording, or by any information
storage and retrieval system, without permission in writing from
the publisher.*
For information address: Bantam Books.

*If you purchased this book without a cover you should be aware that
this book is stolen property. It was reported as "unsold and destroyed"
to the publisher and neither the author nor the publisher has received
any payment for this "stripped book."*

ISBN 0-553-15996-8

Published simultaneously in the United States and Canada

Bantam Books are published by Bantam Books, a division of Bantam Doubleday Dell Publishing Group, Inc. Its trademark, consisting of the words
"Bantam Books" and the portrayal of a rooster, is Registered in U.S. Patent
and Trademark Office and in other countries. Marca Registrada. Bantam
Books, 666 Fifth Avenue, New York, New York 10103.

PRINTED IN THE UNITED STATES OF AMERICA

CWO   0 9 8 7 6 5 4 3 2 1

For Judy,
who helped bring
the Never Sink Nine
into play

CHAPTER ONE

Tony's Turn

Walter Dodd sneaked his bike out of the garage. When his front tire hit the street he jumped on and started pedaling. "Safe." He headed at full speed down Elm Street.

Mrs. Dodd's head popped up from a flower bed. "Walter!" she yelled. "Come back here and help me weed!"

It was too late. Her words were lost in the wind.

Walter turned his baseball cap around backward. It was a perfect day for a swim—

hot and sticky. Grandpa Walt would call it a cotton-candy day. Grandpa Walt was the Never Sink Nine's team coach. He kept in tip-top shape by swimming fifty laps at the YMCA every day.

Walter looked down at his brand-new swimming trunks. They were printed all over with little baseball bats and gloves. He couldn't wait to show his best friend and Never Sink Nine teammate, Mike Lasky.

Walter timed the ride to Mike's house on his official Babe Ruth wristwatch. "Three minutes, twenty-one seconds, exactly," he said, coasting up the Laskys' driveway. It was Sunday and Mike's dad was mowing the lawn.

"Hi, Mr. Lasky." Walter saluted him. Mike's dad was a cop.

Mr. Lasky saluted him back. "Afternoon, Mr. Dodd. Going for a swim?"

Walter nodded. "With Mike," he said, heading for the front door.

"Not today," said Mr. Lasky. "Mike's got a lot of practicing to do before his piano recital Saturday."

Walter stopped and turned around. "He can't! Our team plays the Bug Busters on Saturday. It's our big rematch."

"I know," Mr. Lasky said. He leaned over to take a drink of cold water from the hose. "Mike's not too happy about missing the game, either," he said.

Walter peered into the Laskys' living-room window. Mike was bent over the piano keys playing his scales. He looked hot, and his hair was standing up in patches.

"Can't Mike go for just a quick swim, Mr. Lasky?" begged Walter. "Ple-e-e-e-ease?"

"Afraid not, son," said Mr. Lasky. "I'm sorry." He went back to his mowing.

Walter waited until Mr. Lasky wasn't looking and tapped on the window. Mike turned and shrugged. Walter shrugged back.

Mike started to play "Take Me Out to the

4

Ball Game." Walter forced a smile and waved good-bye.

Walter pedaled slowly to the YMCA. Who would take Mike's place at this week's game? Mike was team shortstop and cleanup hitter, too. He'd have to ask Grandpa Walt about it right away.

Walter parked his bike next to Grandpa Walt's old station wagon and headed for the pool inside. He smelled the chlorine before he saw the water.

"Hi, Walter," said a man sitting behind a counter stacked with towels. It was Mr. Ackerman, who lived at the Y. "Looking for your grandpa?"

Walter nodded.

"You're in the right place. He came in about an hour ago. Had a boy about your age with him."

Walter guessed it was his big brother, Danny. He wondered why Danny hadn't said he was coming with Grandpa Walt today. *I'll surprise them,* thought Walter. He kicked off his right sneaker and picked out two quarters. He gave them to Mr. Ackerman and held out his hand to be stamped.

Walter wished the little black fish stamp wouldn't wash off. It looked like a real tattoo. It made him feel tough.

Walter took a towel from Mr. Ackerman and opened a door marked POOL. Inside, the huge pool was crowded with people swimming laps. Walter took off his T-shirt and dropped it in a pile with his shoes and towel. He dipped a foot in the shallow end. It was warm as bathwater.

Walter spotted his grandfather's head down at the deep end. A smaller head bobbed up and down in the water beside him. There's Danny, thought Walter. I'm really going to surprise them. He crept along the edge of the pool toward the deep end.

Grandpa Walt was hanging on to the side of the pool, talking. Walter took a running start and jumped over their heads. "Geronimo!" he shouted, tucking his body into a

6

cannonball. He hit the water with a loud splash.

"Surprise!" shouted Walter, rocketing up out of the water. He looked straight into the face of Tony Pappas, one of his Never Sink Nine teammates. "What're *you* doing here?" he said, looking around for Danny.

"Great cannonball!" Tony said.

"Hi, sport," said Grandpa Walt. "Tony and I came here to work out."

"Gotta strengthen my leg if I'm gonna play this Saturday," said Tony. "Right, Coach?" He smiled up at Grandpa Walt. Grandpa Walt smiled back and nodded.

Tony had had a broken leg all season. Now his cast was off.

Walter pushed himself between Tony and Grandpa Walt. "Mike can't play this Saturday!"

"No problem," said Grandpa Walt. "Tony can fill in as shortstop."

"But Mike and I always play short and

second," said Walter. "We're the keystone combination."

"It's Tony's turn now," said Grandpa Walt, pulling himself up out of the pool. "Everyone gets a chance to play different positions on our team. You know that, Walt. You pitched just last week." He held out a hand to Tony. Tony grabbed hold and got a free ride up out of the water. It was easy to see which leg had been in a cast. His right leg was a little thinner.

"Sorry we can't stay, slugger," Grandpa Walt said. "I've got to get Tony home. But I'll see you later."

"I have to help out at the store," said Tony. His parents owned Never Sink Plumbers, Inc., their team sponsor.

Walter watched Grandpa Walt and Tony towel off and walk out together.

The lifeguard leaned over the side of the pool toward Walter. "Don't let me catch you doing cannonballs again, kid."

Walter pushed off and swam two laps of

8

his favorite stroke, the Australian crawl. His heart wasn't in it, though. He sat on the edge of the pool and looked at his new swimming trunks. All the colors looked brighter when they were wet. He wished he could show Grandpa Walt or Mike. It was no fun swimming alone.

Walter decided to take a cool shower and head home. In the men's room he found a soap drawing on the mirror—a baseball bat with NEVER SINK NINE written on it.

"Doesn't Tony ever stop drawing?" Walter said to himself. "He'll never be able to play shortstop like Mike. All he can do is take roll call and draw pictures."

Walter took his towel and wiped away Tony's drawing. He'd have to talk to Grandpa Walt about Tony at practice tomorrow. The Never Sink Nine had to win on Saturday. He and Grandpa Walt would find a way.

CHAPTER TWO

Grandpa Walt's Choice

After school Monday Walter and Mike bicycled off the Eleanor Roosevelt Elementary School playground together. Walter pedaled up next to Mike.

"You've got to make team practice today," said Walter. "Or Tony will get your position."

Mike popped a big bubble with his gum. "Can't. I've got to practice for my recital."

"Drop it," said Walter. "Your parents can't make you play the piano."

"I kinda like it," said Mike.

"As much as baseball?" Walter looked amazed.

Mike shrugged.

"Who likes piano as much as baseball!" shouted Walter. "You can't hit a home run on a piano!"

Mike shrugged again and coasted downhill ahead of Walter. "See ya later, alligator!" he shouted back and headed for home.

Walter didn't answer. He pedaled toward Diamond Park. He had to get to Grandpa Walt before Tony showed up.

A few kids were warming up on the Babe Ruth and Mickey Mantle fields. Walter pedaled to the farthest diamond—Willie Mays. It was empty.

"Good," said Walter. "Tony isn't here yet. Grandpa Walt must be in the equipment shed." Walter tossed his backpack into the dugout.

"Ouch!" A voice came from inside the dugout.

Walter bent down and looked inside. At the far end of the bench sat Tony, rubbing his arm. His drawing pad was on his lap. Walter's backpack lay at his feet.

"Sorry." Walter started for the equipment shed. He had to get to Grandpa Walt fast.

"Guess what!" Tony yelled after him. "Coach made me shortstop. I'm playing next to you this Saturday. Isn't that great?"

Walter's heart sank. He turned around and forced himself to smile. "Just great," said Walter.

Grandpa Walt came out of the equipment shed dragging a heavy bag. He waved to Walter. "How about giving your coach a hand?" he shouted.

Walter ran to help him. This was his chance to change Grandpa Walt's mind. He took hold of the bag and started in on Tony. "You can't make Tony shortstop. He hasn't played all season. He's gonna wreck everything. We'll lose the game." He caught his breath and kept going. "Besides, Mike's a great shortstop and—"

"Whoa!" Grandpa Walt held up a hand. "I never said Tony would be shortstop forever, did I?"

Walter looked up at his grandfather and shook his head.

"I thought you liked all your teammates," said Grandpa Walt. He sounded serious.

"I do," said Walter.

"Then why shouldn't Tony get a shot at shortstop?" said Grandpa Walt. "I gave you a chance to pitch. You couldn't even get the ball over the plate at first, remember?"

Walter looked down and dug the toe of his sneaker in the dirt. He wished he'd never said anything.

"Neigh-h-h-h!"

Grandpa Walt and Walter turned to see three girls cantering across the field—Melissa Nichols, her little sister, Jenny, and Katie Kessler.

Walter rolled his eyes. They were *always* pretending to be horses. Melissa even carried a backpack full of plastic horses everywhere she went.

"Ba-a-a-a-a-a!"

A goat wearing a Never Sink Nine baseball cap chased the girls across the field. It was Homer, the team mascot. He belonged to their newest member, Pete Santos.

Pretty soon the whole team was warming up on the Willie Mays field—including Tony.

Grandpa Walt walked onto the pitcher's mound. He blew the whistle hanging around his neck and motioned everyone to gather around him.

"Time for team practice to start," said Tony, jogging past Walter. He sounded excited.

"Big deal," said Walter. But he was as excited as Tony about the big game on Saturday.

First Tony took roll call. Everyone was there. Then Grandpa Walt stepped forward. "I'm afraid I've got bad news," he said. "Mike Lasky won't be able to play shortstop in this week's game."

14

Everyone moaned. Then Grandpa Walt put a hand on Tony's shoulder. "The good news is, Tony's cast is now off and he's taking Mike's place."

Tony smiled up at Grandpa Walt. A couple of kids clapped Tony on the back.

"Unfortunately, last week's game against the Bug Busters was disqualified," said Grandpa Walt.

"We won it fair and square," said Otis Hooper through his catcher's mask.

"Yeah!" everyone echoed.

Grandpa Walt held up his hand until everyone was quiet. "As you know, our team mascot caught the winning fly ball. Goats are not allowed to play—not even Homer."

The brown-and-white goat butted Grandpa Walt gently and licked his hand. Grandpa Walt gave him a pat on the head. "Sorry, old boy," he said.

He turned his attention back to the team.

"The Bug Busters are fighting mad

15

about our rematch this Saturday. We've got a lot of work to do."

Everyone nodded.

"Today we're going to work on hitting. Everyone gets a chance at bat. I've got to choose a cleanup hitter to fill in for Mike."

Walter punched his mitt with his fist. He'd been working on his hitting all weekend with his big brother, Danny. This was his chance to be a real slugger.

"Everyone take the field, except Otis," said Grandpa Walt. "We need our catcher at home plate. I'll pitch today."

Melissa Nichols flicked her ponytail back. She looked disappointed. She was the team's star pitcher and was happiest on the mound.

Grandpa Walt turned toward a long-haired girl wearing pink ballet tights. "Christy, you bat first. Everyone else spread out on the field."

Walter jogged straight for second base, his favorite position. He pretended to swing

16

an invisible bat through the air. "*Swoooooosh!*" he said.

"*Swoooooosh!*" said Tony, pretending to swing a bat, too. He smiled at Walter from Mike's old shortstop position.

Walter looked away. "Copycat," he whispered. But he didn't care about Tony anymore. He was sure to be cleanup hitter at this Saturday's game.

Christy took a couple of practice swings.

"Ready?" asked Grandpa Walt from the pitcher's mound.

Christy nodded. She missed the first two balls.

"Relax and keep your eye on the ball!" said Grandpa Walt.

Walter was anxious to take his turn at bat. He watched Christy hit a foul ball. "I'm better than she is," he told himself. He looked around the field at his teammates. "I'm probably better than all of them."

Christy jogged past Walter into the outfield. "You're next," she said.

17

Walter ran to home plate and strapped on the batting helmet. He ducked into the dugout to get his new Louisville Slugger. Then he pulled up his lucky socks. They had turned a nice dirty blue-gray since Grandpa Walt gave them to him at the start of the season.

"Ready, slugger?" asked Grandpa Walt.

Walter dug in and took a practice swing. "Ready!"

Grandpa Walt threw a slow underhand pitch.

Walter swung around and hit a grounder right to him.

"Good hit," said Grandpa Walt. "This time throw your weight into it. And choke up on your bat."

Walter dug his back foot into the dirt to brace himself. Then he slid his hands a little higher on the bat. He nodded to Grandpa Walt.

"Here comes a fast one." Grandpa Walt wound up. He threw it right over home plate.

Walter swung around fast.

18

Crack! It was a line drive past Grandpa Walt into the outfield.

Walter hit five more balls and missed only one.

"You've been practicing," said Grandpa Walt. "Those Bug Busters won't get anything past you this Saturday."

Walter was bursting with pride. He had worked hard to improve his hitting. He handed the batting helmet to Felix. As Walter jogged past, Grandpa Walt clapped him on the back and winked.

"You're cleanup hitter for sure," Tony said to Walter back on the field. "No contest."

Walter grinned. Maybe Tony wouldn't make such a bad shortstop, after all.

The sun was almost setting. The Bug Busters had finished practice and were watching from the sidelines. The Decker twins were carrying their team mascots—four big jars of black flies.

One of the identical twin brothers waved

at Walter. "Hey, Dodd! Too bad your team slugger wimped out of the rematch!"

"Our slugger's right here!" Tony shouted back and pointed to Walter.

Robert and Richard Decker laughed.

Grandpa Walt took a step toward them. The twins ran off holding their jars of flies.

"Look who's laughing now," said Melissa. She picked up her backpack of toy horses and headed for the dugout. Everyone started to follow her in.

"Wait a minute!" said Grandpa Walt. "One of our team hasn't had a turn at bat yet."

Melissa looked around the field. "Everyone's had a turn."

"Not Tony," said Grandpa Walt.

Tony looked down at his mitt. "That's okay," he said.

Grandpa Walt slipped the helmet on Tony's head and pressed a bat in his hand. "It's not okay," he said, giving him a shove. "You're up, kiddo."

Tony dragged the bat over to home plate.

He swung the bat up over one shoulder and waited for the pitch. Walter moped back to second.

CRACK!

Walter squinted up at the small white ball sailing overhead.

"It's a homer!" shouted Grandpa Walt.

"Wow!" Otis took off his catcher's mask. Everyone watched the ball soar high over the outfield toward the back fence. Only Homer tried to chase after the ball.

Grandpa Walt walked over to Tony and put an arm around his shoulders. "Looks like we've found our new cleanup hitter."

Everyone swarmed around Tony to congratulate him—except Walter. He still couldn't believe it.

"It was a mistake," said Tony. "I'm really not that good." He looked scared.

"Nonsense," said Grandpa Walt. "Now let's get this equipment in the shed before it gets dark. I'll leave Melissa and Walter in charge tonight. I want everyone to practice

hitting and catching at home this week. The Bug Busters play hard, and there won't be any goats catching balls for us this time."

Homer dropped the ball at Grandpa Walt's feet. Grandpa Walt rubbed the goat's velvety nose. "We meet Saturday on the Mickey Mantle field. Ten o'clock, sharp. See you there!" Grandpa Walt dumped the empty equipment bag in Walter's arms.

Tony walked off the field surrounded by his teammates. He turned to wave good-bye to Walter. Walter pretended not to see him.

Melissa started picking up the bases. "Hurry up, Walter!"

Walter slowly dragged the equipment bag over. He still couldn't believe what had happened.

"Look, Walter!" Melissa pointed to two boys creeping into the outfield toward her bag of horses. Her face turned white. She started running toward the Decker twins. "My ponies!" she shouted. "Leave them alone!"

Robert Decker tossed one of the toy

ponies in the air. "This is what our team's gonna do to you on Saturday!" Richard Decker took a swing at it with his bat. The pony broke into two big pieces. The twins ran off the field laughing.

Melissa cradled the small gray spotted horse in her arms. "It's Misty," she said, fighting back tears.

Walter knew Misty was Melissa's favorite. He picked up Misty's broken leg. "Maybe we can fix it," he said.

Melissa shook her head. "When a horse has a broken leg they shoot it."

Tony had a broken leg, thought Walter. I almost wish *he* had been a horse. Then I'd be cleanup hitter.

Walter put an arm around Melissa's shoulders. "We'll get 'em back on Saturday," he said. Melissa picked up her bag of horses. Without saying another word, they walked to the equipment shed.

Walter gave the equipment bag a little

kick and pushed it inside the shed. "A lot of good all that practice did me."

"I'm going to fix those Decker twins," said Melissa.

"How?"

"I'll tell you tomorrow." Melissa made a *V* for victory sign as she started toward home.

CHAPTER THREE

Tony Baloney

Walter ran up the crowded hallway of Eleanor Roosevelt Elementary. He couldn't wait. Today he'd hear Melissa's plan to get back at the Decker twins. He saw Melissa and Christy talking outside their third-grade classroom.

"Wait up, Walter!" Otis yelled from behind him.

Walter stopped short. Otis barreled right into him.

"Oof!" Walter's bat fell out of his backpack and rolled to a stop at Melissa's feet.

Melissa hugged her bag of horses tight. "The Decker twins are going to be sorry they hurt Misty." Her green eyes narrowed. "Tony and I have a plan."

Walter picked up his Louisville Slugger. "What plan?"

"It's a secret between Tony and me," said Melissa. "You'll find out at lunchtime." She flicked her ponytail and walked into Mrs. Howard's room.

Otis took a bite out of his candy bar and rolled his eyes at Walter. Walter shrugged. The boys slowly followed the girls into the classroom.

Inside everyone was sharpening pencils, putting things in desks, and getting ready for the day. Mrs. Howard sat at her desk correcting papers with her red pencil.

Pete Santos was writing his daily joke on the blackboard. Every day he wrote a new one. Finding the answer was a treasure hunt. He always left the answer in a different spot.

"Finished." Pete put down the chalk.

TUESDAY - Pete's joke
of the day
What do you get when you
cross Tony with a
sandwich?

Walter looked up at the board.

"You mean Tony Pappas?" asked Walter.

"The one and only," said Pete.

Walter grinned. Pete was making fun of Tony. "Where'd you leave the answer?" He couldn't wait to see it.

"In the cafeteria," said Pete. "Taped under the red table."

Walter headed for the door.

Mrs. Howard looked up from her desk. "Not now, Walter. School starts in five minutes. You'll have to wait until lunch." Her big daisy earrings swished from side to side.

Walter took his seat. He didn't think he

28

could wait until lunch to find out Melissa's plan and the answer to Pete's joke.

Students were starting to fill up the desks. Everyone was talking about Tony's home-run hit. Walter's ears started to burn. He put his hands over his ears.

Suddenly Mike Lasky burst through the door. He went over to Mrs. Howard and bent his head down. A pink blob was stuck in his hair.

Mrs. Howard took one look, sighed, and got out her scissors.

Walter waited while Mrs. Howard clipped the sticky gum out of Mike's hair. It happened about once a week. Mike loved the gum that came from packs of baseball cards. He had the biggest collection in the third grade.

"Thanks, Mrs. Howard." Mike rubbed the newly clipped patch on top of his head.

Mrs. Howard stood up and clapped her hands. "Everybody please take your seat."

Mike hurried to his desk beside Walter.

"I've got to talk to you at lunch," Walter

29

whispered to Mike. Walter looked at his Babe Ruth wristwatch—8:02. He figured the time until lunch. "Three hours and twenty-eight minutes more," he whispered. It was going to be a long morning.

At eleven-thirty the lunch bell rang. Mrs. Howard's class raced down the hall to the cafeteria—all except Pete. He already knew the answer to his joke.

Otis Hooper plowed through the crowded cafeteria to the red table. He squeezed underneath it. Everyone gathered around. They could hear Otis chuckling under the table.

"Come on, Otis." Melissa tapped her foot impatiently. "What's the punch line?"

Pete's joke went through Walter's head. *What do you get when you cross Tony with a sandwich?*

Otis backed out from under the table. His round face was red from laughing. He held up a piece of paper.

Everyone laughed, but Walter laughed the hardest. "Wait till Tony sees this," he said.

TONY BALONEY

Just then Tony walked over to the table. "What's so funny?"

"Pete's joke." Otis snickered. "What do you get when you cross Tony with a sandwich?" He held up the paper. "Tony Baloney. Get it?"

Walter waited for Tony to get mad and walk off. But he just smiled. Then he laughed. "Tony Baloney, that's me!"

How stupid can you get? He's laughing at himself, thought Walter.

Everyone laughed along with Tony. Then they all sat down at the lunch table.

Tony propped up his drawing pad for everyone to see. "Look," he said.

Everyone stared at three empty boxes lined up in a row.

"What's *Sidelines*?" asked Mike.

"It's the name of the Never Sink Nine's

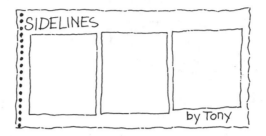

own comic strip," said Tony. "I'm going to make one for every game we play."

"That's dumb," muttered Walter.

Melissa frowned at Walter. "You're just jealous."

"Tony can't draw and play baseball, too," blurted out Walter.

"Why not?" said Christy. "I play baseball and I'm a ballerina. Mike likes to play piano and he's on the team, too."

Mike blushed. He liked Christy.

"You can be pretty dumb sometimes, Walter," said Christy.

Walter's ears started to burn. He felt like punching someone. But mostly he just wished he could disappear.

32

"Uh-oh." Otis slunk down in his seat. "Here come the Decker twins."

Robert and Richard Decker stood over their table grinning. They each had a front tooth missing. "Hello, Never *Stink* Nine," said Richard.

"Bug off, Bug Busters!" Melissa shot back.

"How about a little dessert first?" asked Richard. He reached into his pocket and tossed a handful of spiders, ants, and worms onto the table. Everyone screamed and stood up.

Melissa picked up one of the plastic spiders. "They're fake!"

Walter saw Melissa give a nod toward Tony.

Tony leapt up and went over to the cafeteria bulletin board. "Hey, everyone!" he announced. "Come look at the Decker twins cartoon!"

A few kids went over to the bulletin board. They started laughing. A crowd

33

gathered quickly. Everyone was laughing.

"What's so funny?" Robert Decker pushed his way to the front of the crowd. His twin brother followed.

The next thing Walter knew the twins were racing out of the cafeteria with bright red faces.

"That'll teach 'em," said Melissa. She gave Tony a high five.

Walter and the rest of the Never Sink Nine walked over to the bulletin board. Pinned to it was a big cartoon drawing of the Decker twins with a joke.

The team burst out laughing. Even Walter couldn't hold back.

Pete clapped Tony on the back. "Good one, Tony Baloney."

"A picture's worth a thousand words," said Christy.

The Never Sink Nine walked out to the playground together to practice hitting.

"Come on, Walter!" shouted Mike.

Walter lagged behind. Tony was Grandpa

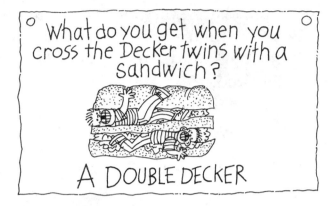

Walt's pet, the new cleanup batter, and he could draw funny cartoons. Couldn't Tony do *anything* wrong?

CHAPTER FOUR

Number Nineteen

Walter pushed up one sleeve and made a muscle. He turned toward Grandpa Walt at the Dodds' dinner table. "Go on," he dared. "Feel it." He'd been doing push-ups all week.

Grandpa Walt gave Walter's arm a light squeeze. His eyes opened wide. "Killer muscles!" He shrank back as if he were afraid. "I'd better watch out for you."

Walter smiled proudly. Grandpa Walt always knew what to say.

37

"Killer schmiller," said Walter's older brother, Danny. "The only thing he ever killed was a fly." Danny flicked a pea across the table at Walter.

Walter ducked and shot back with a cherry tomato. He wasn't going to let Danny ruin tonight. Grandpa Walt came to dinner every Friday night. It was the only time all week Walter didn't have to share him with the whole team.

"Since you boys have so much energy," said Mrs. Dodd, "you can clear the table and wash the dishes."

Walter and Danny let out a loud groan.

"You heard your mother," said Mr. Dodd. "And let's have no more throwing food around."

Grandpa Walt gave Walter a wink. "See you after kitchen duty."

Walter and Danny finished the dishes in record time. Danny sat down to watch his favorite TV show. Walter raced outside to find

Grandpa Walt. He was working under the hood of Mr. Dodd's car. Walter tugged on his shirt.

"Let's play catch," said Walter. The rematch was tomorrow and Walter wanted to practice.

"In a little while," said Grandpa Walt. "I'm giving your dad's car a tune-up." Grandpa Walt had been a bus driver for thirty years. He loved working on cars.

"Can I help?" asked Walter.

"Not here," said Grandpa Walt. "But I have an errand you could do."

"Sure."

Grandpa Walt walked over to his station wagon and pulled out a brand-new Never Sink Nine team shirt. "Take this over to Tony's house. I had his new team number put on for tomorrow's game."

Walter's eyes opened wide. He stared at the pale blue number. "Nineteen!" he shouted. "That's your old number!"

"Right," said Grandpa Walt. "Back when I played in the minors with the North Dakota Nine."

"You can't give him your number!" said Walter.

"Why not?" asked Grandpa Walt.

"Because," said Walter, trying to think of a reason. "Because I want it!"

"You have the number you said you wanted," said Grandpa Walt. "Number two, Danny's number."

Walter couldn't think of anything to say. It was true. He had wanted the same number as his big brother. "Tony can't have it," said Walter softly. "You're *my* grandfather."

Grandpa Walt put an arm around Walter's shoulders and gave him a squeeze. "Tony's had a hard time with his broken leg. He's got a lot of heart. Even when he couldn't play he never gave up being part of the team." He gave Walter a little push toward his bike. "We'll play when you get back."

Walter moped over to his bike. He didn't

41

care about playing catch anymore. He didn't even care about the game tomorrow. Grandpa Walt had given Tony his old team number. Nothing else mattered.

Walter pushed off and headed for downtown Rockville. He stuffed part of the team shirt in his jeans pocket. It trailed out in the wind. "I hope it falls out and a truck runs over it," said Walter. But it didn't.

Walter turned up Main Street and parked in front of Never Sink Plumbers, Inc. Tony lived behind the store with his family.

Walter walked around back and knocked on the door. A dark-haired man wearing overalls answered.

"Hi, Mr. Pappas," said Walter. "Is Tony home?"

Mr. Pappas opened the door wide. "Come in, Walter, come in. Tony will be happy to see a teammate."

Walter followed Mr. Pappas into the kitchen. Tony was sitting at the table with a lot of small children.

"Walter!" Tony jumped up.

Walter held out the team shirt. "Here."

Tony pulled it on over his T-shirt. "How does it look?"

Tony's younger brothers and sisters gathered around. Walter wondered what it was like to be the oldest instead of a little brother.

"Let's go to my room," said Tony. "It's quieter."

"I've got to go," said Walter.

"But I made a drawing for Coach," said Tony.

"He doesn't want it," Walter lied.

"It's of you and Coach together." Tony sounded hurt.

Walter looked down at the floor. "Okay."

Tony led Walter back into a tiny room with no windows. The walls were covered with Tony's drawings. "This is my room," said Tony. He took a drawing down from the wall and handed it to Walter. "Here."

The boy in the picture wore his baseball

cap backward, just like Walter. The man was big and had a mustache and glasses, like Grandpa Walt.

"It's good," said Walter. He looked at an old photo taped to the wall above Tony's bed. An old man in a baseball cap had his arm around Tony. Tony looked younger. They were both smiling.

"That's my *pappous*," said Tony, softly.

"What's a *pappous*?" asked Walter.

"It's Greek for grandfather," said Tony. "My *pappous* is dead."

"Oh." Walter didn't know what to say. He had never known anyone who had died. He couldn't imagine life without Grandpa Walt.

"You're lucky you still have yours," said Tony. "We used to play catch. We'd pretend we were doing a double play together. I miss him."

"I've seen my brother do a double play," said Walter. "He's Danny the Driver. He's the best hitter on his team. He gives me pointers sometimes."

Tony picked up a bat leaning against a corner. "Can you teach me to hit before tomorrow?"

Walter grinned. Who was Tony fooling? "You're the new cleanup batter."

"I'm lousy," said Tony. He looked scared. "My hit was just an accident."

"Sure," said Walter, going along with the joke. "But I only have time for a couple of balls. I've got to get home."

Walter followed Tony into their backyard. He pulled on Tony's mitt and watched him get ready to hit. Tony was leaning way over. He swung the bat over his shoulder like a sack of flour.

Walter chuckled. "What a joker." He wound up and threw a fast one.

Tony swung so hard he spun around in a circle. The bat went flying.

"Very funny," said Walter. "Try hanging on to the bat this time."

"Okay," said Tony. He picked up the bat and held it so tight his knuckles turned white.

45

Walter tossed a soft underhand ball.

Tony swung before the ball reached him.

"Stop fooling around," said Walter.

Tony lowered the bat. "I'm not." His voice cracked and he looked away. "Maybe you were right. I can't draw and play baseball, too."

Walter's mouth dropped open. Tony wasn't kidding. He walked over to him. "Why didn't you tell anyone?"

"I did," said Tony.

Walter remembered Tony had said at practice that his hit was just a lucky hit. "We didn't believe it," he said.

"I'm gonna wreck the game," said Tony.

"You'll be okay," said Walter. "I'll help." He tried to remember all the tips Grandpa Walt had told him. "Remember to keep your eye on the ball." He grabbed the bat and showed Tony how to hold it. "Stand with your feet apart and bend your knees. Hold the bat out from your body like this. Take a short step toward the pitcher and push with your back

46

foot. Keep your shoulders level and follow through."

Tony nodded.

By the time Walter left it was getting dark and Tony looked hopeful.

Walter bicycled home with Tony's drawing of him and Grandpa Walt in his pocket. "I have to warn Grandpa Walt about Tony," said Walter, pedaling faster.

Walter coasted down Elm Street into his driveway. Danny was sitting on the front lawn. Grandpa Walt's old station wagon was gone.

"Grandpa Walt said he'd see you at the game," said Danny. "He couldn't wait any longer. Tough luck, turkey brain."

Walter was so worried he didn't bother to get mad. "Why didn't he wait for me?" said Walter. "Now we'll lose for sure."

CHAPTER FIVE

Cleanup Hitter

On Saturday Walter woke up with two things on his mind: breakfast and getting to Grandpa Walt before their game with the Bug Busters.

"I have to warn him!" said Walter, leaping out of bed.

"Huh?" Danny rolled over. He opened one eye. "Warn who?"

"Grandpa Walt!" Walter smoothed down his Never Sink Nine uniform. He always wore it to bed the night before a game. "He doesn't know our cleanup hitter can't even hit!" Walter stepped across the line of tape dividing their room in half.

Danny raised his head from the pillow and sniffed the air. He saw Walter pulling the dirty blue-gray socks out of his cap. "Hey, did you put those stinko socks in my cap again?"

Walter froze. "I had to, for extra luck," he said.

Danny looked down at Walter's feet. "What do you think you're doing on *my* side of the room!" He reached under his pillow and pulled out a black water pistol.

"No!" screamed Walter. A stream of water splashed his face. He grabbed his baseball gear and dashed for the door.

Walter skipped breakfast to save time. He started for Grandpa Walt's apartment in downtown Rockville. It was on the second floor above Christy Chung's family's restaurant.

Walter parked his bike in front of Chung's Restaurant and pushed the intercom buzzer.

"Who's there?" asked a voice over the loudspeaker. It was Grandpa Walt.

"It's me, Grandpa," said Walter.

"Come on up," said Grandpa Walt. There was a buzzing noise, and Walter pushed the door open. He climbed the stairs, two at a time.

Grandpa Walt stood at his open door. He was still in his pajamas. "What brings you over so bright and early?"

Walter followed the smell of bacon into the kitchen. His stomach rumbled. He forgot all about Tony. "Can I have some breakfast?" he asked.

Grandpa Walt set a place for Walter. They sat down to a breakfast of orange juice, toast, bacon, and eggs. Grandpa Walt looked at the kitchen clock. "I better get going, or we'll be late for the game." He headed for the bathroom and turned on the shower.

The game! Suddenly Walter remembered why he had come.

"Tony can't hit!" he shouted. He raced into the steamy bathroom.

Grandpa Walt poked his head outside the shower curtain. "What?"

"Tony's homer at practice was an accident!" said Walter. He was hopping up and down. "He can't hit! He can't hit at all!"

A line of worry creased Grandpa Walt's forehead. "Are you sure?"

"We practiced in his yard last night," said Walter. "He couldn't even hold the bat right."

Grandpa Walt sighed and shut the curtain. Walter sat on the toilet seat waiting for an answer. Grandpa Walt turned off the water, grabbed a towel, and stepped out.

"Well?" Walter said impatiently. "What are we going to do?"

Grandpa Walt began lathering his face in front of the mirror. "About what?"

"Tony!" Walter stood up.

"Nothing." Grandpa Walt shaved his face in long, clean strokes.

Walter couldn't believe his ears. "We'll lose the game," he said.

"Maybe," said Grandpa Walt. He turned to Walter. "What do you suggest we do?"

Walter smiled. He had been waiting for this moment. "I could be the cleanup hitter," he said with a grin.

"You could," said Grandpa Walt, patting his face dry. "But this is Tony's turn at bat. Win or lose, the batting lineup stays the same."

Walter could tell by the sound of Grandpa Walt's voice that he meant it. Without another word they loaded Walter's bike into the station wagon and drove to Diamond Park. Everyone was warming up on the Mickey Mantle field—including the Bug Busters.

Melissa came cantering up to Walter with a can of bug spray. "The field's full of flies today," she said. "Cover your eyes and close your mouth."

Walter obeyed and Melissa sprayed him from head to foot. She cantered off around the field spraying every one of the Never Sink Nine.

"Why don't you warm up with the rest of the team?" Grandpa Walt said to Walter. "I have to talk to the Bug Busters' coach."

Walter jogged out to Tony at shortstop. "Hi, Tony."

Tony forced a nervous smile. "Would you take my place at bat?" he pleaded.

Walter bit his lip. He wanted to take Tony's place as cleanup hitter more than anything. "Grandpa Walt won't let me," he answered.

Tony sighed and gave the ground a kick.

"Heads up!" Otis hit a fast ground ball from home plate.

Walter barely had time to look up. In one fast move Tony caught Otis's ball and shot it all the way back to him at home plate.

"Nice catch!" yelled Otis. "Good arm!" He hit some more grounders to the infield and Tony caught every one. He was like a vacuum cleaner. He scooped them up as fast as Otis hit them.

"Wow!" yelled Pete. "Where'd you learn that?"

Tony shrugged. "My *pappous* taught me. And I practiced a lot when my leg was broken."

Walter was impressed. He'd never seen anyone throw so fast except on TV.

Felix ran past Walter and Tony into the outfield. "The Bug Busters are at bat first!" he shouted back at them.

Walter heard Tony breathe a sigh of relief. "I wish we could stay out here the whole game," Tony said.

Walter nodded from second base.

The Bug Busters got off to a strong start with two runs.

The Never Sink Nine were working together as a team. They finally fielded three outs.

"Good job," Grandpa Walt said as their team jogged into the dugout. It was the bottom of the first inning and the Never Sink Nine were up to bat.

Grandpa Walt read the batting lineup. "We'll start off with Pete," he said. "Then Christy, Walter, and Tony."

"Our cleanup hitter," said Melissa, smiling at Tony.

Tony picked up his drawing pad and scribbled nervously.

Pete gave Homer a hug and grabbed a bat.

Richard Decker was waiting on the pitcher's mound. "Hurry up, BA-A-A-A-AT-TER!" said Richard. He crooked a finger on either side of his head like Homer's horns.

Pete stomped up to the plate. He didn't like jokes about Homer. He took wild swings at the first two balls.

"Simmer down," said Grandpa Walt. "Concentrate on the game."

Pete planted his feet firmly behind home plate. "Ready," he said.

"BA-A-A-A-ATTER UP!" said Richard again. He laughed as he wound up for the final pitch.

Pete swung before the ball reached him.

"Good try," said Grandpa Walt.

Pete sank down on the bench and hugged Homer.

Christy was next. She hit a fly ball to center field.

"Out!" shouted the umpire as one of the Bug Busters caught it.

"You're next," said Grandpa Walt. He gave Walter a thumbs-up sign.

Walter gave his lucky socks a hard yank and jogged out to home plate. He lifted the bat and took a practice swing. "Hit, hit, hit, hit, hit," he whispered five times. Five was his lucky number. A nice fat one came sailing toward his bat. Walter swung around to meet it.

Crack! A line drive into the outfield!

"Run!" shouted Walter's teammates.

Walter tossed his bat down, flew around first, and headed for second. He slid into second base, feet first.

"Safe!" shouted the umpire.

Walter stood up, grinning. His pants legs were streaked with dirt. He smiled at his teammates in the dugout. He had hit a double. Now all they needed was for their cleanup hitter to hit him home. Walter watched Tony drag his bat toward home plate. His heart sank. Everyone on the team was cheering.

"Come on, Tony!" shouted Melissa. "Hit him home!"

"Get mean with the stick!" said Otis.

Tony swung so hard at the first ball, the bat flew out of his hands. When he swung at the next ball his bat looked like a flyswatter. He stood still and watched the third ball go past.

"Strike three!" said the umpire. "You're out!"

The team crowded around Tony as they took the field.

"Why didn't you tell us you couldn't hit?" demanded Melissa.

"Yeah," said Otis. "We need a *real* cleanup hitter, not a phony."

"I *tried* to tell you," said Tony.

The Never Sink Nine wouldn't listen. They trudged out to their field positions. Tony lagged behind.

"Hey, Tony!" Walter jogged over to him. "Maybe you aren't so hot at bat, but you're *great* at fielding balls."

"So what," Tony mumbled.

"*So*, we're the keystone combination," said Walter. "Maybe we'll even get to do a double play like your *pappous* taught you."

"Think so?" Tony forced a smile. Walter could tell he didn't believe it.

Walter took his position at second. He felt bad for his teammate. *Grandpa Walt was right*, he thought. Tony had heart. He never

59

stopped trying when he had a broken leg or when the whole team turned against him.

But was heart enough to win the game without a cleanup hitter?

CHAPTER SIX

Pappous's Double Play

It was the top of the last inning. The Never Sink Nine was ahead.

"Look at the score!" Pete shouted from first base.

	1	2	3	4	5	6	T
BUGBUSTERS	2	0	1	1	0		4
NEVER SINK NINE	0	1	2	0	2		5

Walter looked up at the scoreboard and smiled. He had hit the last run in himself. "If we can keep 'em from scoring now we'll win!" Walter shouted back to Pete.

Pete didn't hear. He had stuffed his ears with cotton so he couldn't hear the Decker twins make fun of Homer. It had worked. He had batted in two runs. Melissa and Katie batted in runs, too. And Tony managed to get his bat on the ball—even though it was a foul ball.

Grandpa Walt jogged onto the field. The Never Sink Nine crowded around him. "You're playing a great game," he said. "We've got 'em where we want 'em. Just keep cool and cover your positions." It was his last-minute pep talk.

The Never Sink Nine gave each other high fives and took their field positions. The first Bug Buster stepped up to bat.

Otis squatted behind home plate. He gave Melissa the signal for a fastball—one finger pointed down.

Melissa nodded from the pitcher's mound.

62

She wound up and released the ball with a quick snap of her wrist.

Swoooooooosh!

The bat cut through the air too late. The ball was already tucked inside Otis's mitt.

"Strike one!" called the umpire from behind Otis.

"Easy out," said Melissa so the Bug Busters could hear.

Grandpa Walt frowned at her from the Never Sink Nine dugout.

Walter could see the Decker twins squirming on the bench. He knew they couldn't wait to bat.

The batter missed the next two balls.

"Out!" called the umpire.

Richard Decker stomped out to home plate. He ripped the batting helmet off his teammate's head. "You blew it!" he said, grabbing the bat. "Try and get one by me."

Otis signaled three fingers down—a let-up pitch.

Melissa nodded and wound up as if she

was going to throw a fastball. At the last second she threw it slow.

Swish!

Expecting a fastball, Richard swung before the ball reached the plate.

Richard's teammates laughed at him. Walter was glad the Never Sink Nine never laughed at him when he missed.

Richard gripped the bat tighter and hit a single.

"Come on, Robert!" he yelled to his brother from first base. "Hit me home!"

Robert Decker stepped into the batter's box and took a practice swing.

SWOOOOOOSH!

He was a powerhouse hitter.

Walter and Tony exchanged a nervous glance.

Richard yelled to his brother again from first base. "Come on, Robert!"

Robert narrowed his eyes at Melissa. "Hurry up, Ponytail!"

Melissa flicked her ponytail angrily.

"Take your time!" shouted Grandpa Walt.

Walter crouched down and punched his mitt with his fist. He saw Tony do the same out of the corner of his eye. They had to stop this ball.

Melissa took a deep breath and threw a sizzler right over home plate. Robert swung around to meet the ball.

Crack!

A hot grounder headed straight for Tony at shortstop. Tony charged the ball and dropped down on one knee. In one swift motion he scooped up the ball and turned to toss it to Walter on second.

"*Pappous* play!" he shouted.

Walter caught the ball and tagged Richard out as he was sliding into second. He spun around and fired the ball to Pete on first.

Smack! Pete caught the ball in his glove and beat out Robert running to first.

"Three out! Double play!" shouted the umpire. "Good teamwork, kids!"

65

"We did it." Tony stood there, stunned. "We won."

Pete and Walter tossed their mitts in the air and rushed Tony together. All three of them fell to the ground laughing. The rest of the Never Sink Nine crowded around them.

"Where did you kids pick up the double play?" asked Grandpa Walt.

Walter threw an arm around Tony's shoulder. "Tony."

"Yay, Tony!" shouted the team. Grandpa Walt lifted Tony up on his shoulders and carried him back into the dugout.

Christy jumped to one side and started a team cheer.

> "Who's the star of double play,
> Tony, Tony, it's your day!
> Ya-a-a-a-y, Tony!"

Suddenly they heard shouting from the Bug Busters' dugout. Richard and Robert Decker were having a fight.

"Why'd you hit a grounder?" shouted Richard to his twin.

"Why didn't *you* run faster!" Robert shouted back.

Richard Decker picked up a bat. "You should have hit it like this!" He swung the bat around. It flew out of his hands and into the dugout. All four jars of bug mascots crashed to the ground. Hundreds of big black flies swarmed over the Bug Busters' dugout.

Otis lifted his catcher's mask to see better. "Look! Their team mascots are loose!"

The Never Sink Nine laughed as the Bug Busters scrambled out of their dugout. Swarms of flies chased them off the field.

"How come those flies aren't bugging us?" asked Felix.

Melissa held up a can of bug spray and smiled. "I bugproofed us."

Homer licked a fly off his nose.

Grandpa Walt took a team photo. Walter, Tony, and Pete stood up together in front. Everyone helped put the equipment away and then piled into Grandpa Walt's station wagon.

Grandpa Walt honked his horn. "Next stop, the Pizza Palace!"

It was Tony's turn to choose the toppings on the pizza. He chose mushrooms, pepperoni, and feta cheese. While everyone was eating Tony drew his comic strip of today's game. When he finished he pushed the cartoon into the center of the table and took a big bite of pizza.

Everyone laughed as they passed the comic strip around the table.

"This is great," Walter said to Tony. "Will you draw one of our next game, too?"

"Sure," said Tony. "Who're we playing next?"

"The Hawks and the Vampires," said Grandpa Walt. "We play *two* games next week."

Otis stuck out his teeth and flapped his arms like bat wings. "Vampires love pizza!" He grabbed the last piece.

Grandpa Walt walked to the door. "Bus now boarding for home!" he announced.

Grandpa Walt drove everyone home. He always dropped Walter off last. He handed Walter his backpack. "I'm proud of you for helping your teammate."

Walter gave Grandpa Walt a good-bye hug.

Mrs. Dodd met Walter at the front door. "Mike's on the phone," she said.

Walter dumped his backpack and raced

into the den. He picked up the phone. "Hi."

"How'd the game go?" asked Mike.

Walter sank into the sofa. "We won." He told Mike about the Decker twins and the *pappous* double play and the flies getting loose.

Mike laughed. "My recital went great, too. Want to hear?"

"Sure." Walter heard a bump as Mike set the phone down on the piano. He lay back on the sofa and listened to Mike play "Take Me Out to the Ball Game."

"You're really good," Walter said. "Sounds like you *can* hit a home run on a piano." It was fun sharing the day with Mike—even if they hadn't been in the game together.

"Who do we play next?" asked Mike.

"Two games," said Walter. "The Hawks and the Vampires. You'll be back then."

"Yeah," said Mike. "The old keystone combination, back in business again!"

About the Author

GIBBS DAVIS was born in Milwaukee, Wisconsin, and was graduated from the University of California at Berkeley. Her first novel, *Maud Flies Solo,* is also a Bantam Skylark book. She has published *Swann Song,* a young adult novel, with Avon Books. *Walter's Lucky Socks, Major-League Melissa, Slugger Mike, Pete the Magnificent,* and *Tony's Double Play* are all part of the Never Sink Nine series for First Skylark. Gibbs divides her time between New York City and Wisconsin.

About the Illustrator

GEORGE ULRICH was born in Morristown, New Jersey, and received his Bachelor of Fine Arts degree from Syracuse University. He has illustrated several Bantam Skylark books, including *Make Four Million Dollars by Next Thursday!* by Stephen Manes and *The Amazing Adventure of Me, Myself, and I* by Jovial Bob Stine. He lives in Marblehead, Massachusetts, with his wife and two sons.

A BANTAM FIRST SKYLARK

FUN ADVENTURES FROM FIRST SKYLARK!

☐ **SON OF FURRY**

by Jovial Bob Stine, illustrated by Heidi Petach

Furry, the class gerbil, is Eugene and Gordon's project for the big Science Fair. But while the boys are cleaning Furry's cage, the speedy gerbil escapes! Now they need a super-special plan to find him—or something that looks like Furry—before someone notices he's gone!

0-553-15854-6 $2.75/$3.25 in Canada

☐ **THE MUFFIN FIEND**

Written and illustrated by Daniel Pinkwater

A muffin thief is on the loose. Inspector LeChat knows that the only man who can stop this awful criminal is Wolfgang Amadeus Mozart. But can they catch the sneaky pastry thief before there are no muffins left anywhere in Europe?

0-553-15544-X $2.75/$3.25 in Canada

☐ **THE BLUE–NOSED WITCH**

by Margaret Embry, illustrated by Carl Rose

While on her way to a witches' meeting, a very young witch named Blanche spies a group of kids and swoops down for a trick-or-treat adventure beyond her wildest dreams.

0-553-15435-4 $2.75/$3.25 in Canada

Buy them wherever paperback books are sold—or order below:

Bantam Books, Dept. SK-42, 414 East Golf Road, Des Plaines, IL 60016

Please send me the items I have checked above. I am enclosing $_____ (please ad $2.50 to cover postage and handling). Send check or money order, no cash or C.O.D.s please.

Mr/Ms _____

Address_____

City/State_____ Zip _____

SK 42-6/91

Please allow four to six weeks delivery.
Prices and availability subject to change without notice.